# Red Spotted Ned

## Written by Chris Jones, Illustrated by Sarah Marsh

First published 2021 by Yearn to Learn Children's Books

ISBN 978-0-9574392-5-2

# Red Spotted Ned

Dear Mums, Dads, Grandparents...

We really hope your family loves our story of Red Spotted Ned. If it helps turn a few red spots into green ones, then we'll be very happy!

Our mission is to write and draw 12 unique rhyming picture books in 2021. We believe passionately in the power of reading - for all ages. So the potential to create positive impressions on curious young minds is why we're doing it.

But getting seen as a newbie indie author is so hard! Your help would be really welcome. So, if you bought this on Amazon, please leave us a review – they mean the world to us.

We now have a website - yearntolearn.co.uk and a Facebook page (@yearntolearnbooks) where you can discover what we're doing next. A Facebook like would be great and a share amongst your friends would be awesome!

Thank you so much, Chris and Sarah x

ON a little tiny lane,
    in a tiny little town.
Lives an angry Monster,
    and he wears a GIANT Frown!

WHEN HE'S AT HIS MADDEST,
HE'S A SHADE OF FLAMING RED.
SO IT'LL COME AS NO SURPRISE TO LEARN,
HIS NAME'S 'RED SPOTTED NED'.

BUT WHEN HE'S NOT SO ANGRY,
WHICH IS SELDOM EVER SEEN.
THOSE red SPOTS TURN INTO,
a LOVELY SHADE OF green.

WHAT HAS WREAKED HIS WRATH THIS TIME?
WHO HAS FIRED HIS FURY?
AS SO OFTEN IS THE CASE,
it'S HIS NEXT-door NEighbour Yuri.

7

FROM the WINDOW OF HIS KiTCHEN,
HE LOOKS OUT every day.
BUT YURi'S GROWing SUNFLOWErS,
NOW they're getting in the Way.

ALL the things that Make HiM cross,
No Longer iN HiS view.
"Well, no you don't," old Ned FuMed,
"you'll get WHat you are due".

Every day at 1 o'clock,
    Yuri does his shopping.
Ned took his chance, skipped the hedge,
    and began to do some chopping.

10

CLICK...CRUNCH, STALK by STALK,
those SUNFLOWERs Were No More.

AND WHEN HE'd doNE, to MAKE HiS POiNT,
NED LEFT THEM at HiS door.

He stomped and trudged, satisfied
now nothing's in his way.
Things were back to normal in
his life so dull and grey.

THEN THAT NIGHT, WHILE NED'S IN bed,
a gHoULie gHoST appears.
AND gHoULie gHoSTS, as We all KNoW,
are MoNSTerS' greatest FearS!

Teeth a chattered, toes a curled,
He hid beneath the sheet.
In a flash, a hand popped out,
and began to tickle his feet.

He reached up to his table,
to grab some prayer beads.
Said Ghoulie in a fearsome voice,
"I'm the ghost of your bad deeds."

"I'M here tonight to help you learn
the error of your ways."
'pfft' came a cloud of smoke,
and a vision through the haze.

16

It was Yuri coming home to find
his flowers, sad and dying.
He dropped his bags in total shock,
and then Ned saw him crying.

Ned just shrugged his shoulders.
"Well, he blocked my line of vision."
The ghost looked on in disbelief,
then made a quick decision.

ANother puff of smoke creates
a Memory long ago.
Yuri's planting sunflower seeds,
"Oh, I really hope they grow!"

"I hope they cheer up my friend Ned,
poor sad and lonely fellow."
All this time, Ned's spots were red,
but now they're turning yellow.

A third and final puff of smoke,
then one last memory.
It happened just some hours ago,
and one that Ned must see.

YURi'S iN HiS KiTCHEN,
    HE'S getting ready to bake.
    "Ned MiGHT NOT LiKE MY SUNFLOWERS,
    but everyone LoveS cake!"

His task complete, his job was done,
Ghoulie disappears.
Leaving Ned, lying in his bed,
Welling up with tears.

The morning comes and Ned gets up,
He's feeling kind of weird.
And through his front door window sees,
a parcel has appeared.

He looks around, no one in sight,
So quickly takes it in.
Can you believe what's inside ...?
A cake inside a tin!

Ned looks out from his window,
He's no longer feeling mean.
And when he looks down at his feet,
His spots have all turned green.

He goes to cut a slice of cake,
"Hang on Ned!" he declared.
"You're going to need two slices now,
because cake is better shared".

In a tiny little town,
    Sits a little tiny lane.
And the Monster you will find there,
    is happy once again.

THE END

We're on a mission to write 12 rhyming picture books in 12 months …
and we'd love you to come on the journey with us!

Check out our other amazing books available now…

## Princess Pea of Popty Ping

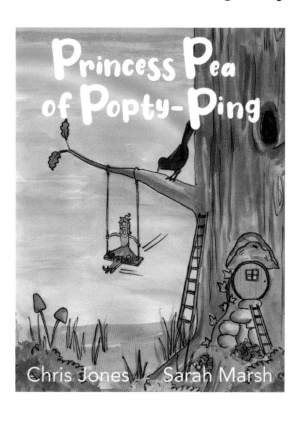

Princess Penelope is not like you and me.
　　She used to live in an old oak tree.
But then she uprooted, which was a curious thing,
　　because now her address is Popty-Ping.

## Harley Hound

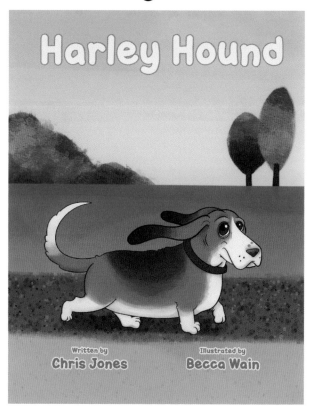

Harley's not like other dogs,
　　she's called a basset hound.
Her butt goes left when she goes right,
　　with ears that sweep the ground.

Coming soon from this author...

# Myrtle the Hawksbill Turtle

Did you know there are only around 700 hawksbill turtles left on the planet? This beautiful and heart-warming story introduces the impact of climate change and conservation, but in a gentle & upbeat way.

Here's some snippets...

On the shores of Costa Rica,
    lives a gorgeous hawksbill turtle.
And if you've ever seen her,
    you'll know her name is Myrtle.

Her shell is quite amazing,
    its parts are called a scute.
A blend of awesome colours,
    that make her look...a beaut!

Visit us at yearntolearn.co.uk or search for our books on Amazon.

# Bessie Bibbs' Ginormous Fibs!

The second book in our monster series. This time we meet Bessie. She just can't help but tell fibs. And whilst her intentions are good, they keep getting her into trouble ...
with very messy consequences!

In the town of Biggle Wiggle,
    lives the monster, Bessie Bibbs.
And all this lady wants to do,
    is tell ginormous fibs!

The type of fibbers we might know,
    tell stories wide and tall.
But Bessie's one of those you'd call,
    a blessed know-it-all!

Printed in Great Britain
by Amazon